Longfellow

And The Deep Hidden Woods

We hope you enjoy
our book

Richard
🐾

English Version ISBN: 978-1-61098-344-0; E-Book 978-1-61098-345-7
French Version ISBN: 978-1-61098-346-4; E-Book 978-161098-347-1
Spanish Version ISBN: 978-1-61098-348-8; E-Book 978-1-61098-349-4

Published by: Hush Puppy Books – TNPC ® Las Vegas NV 89109

PUBLISHER'S NOTE
Longfellow and The Deep Hidden Woods is a work of fiction created wholly by Dr. Richard Wagner's imagination.
All characters are fictional and any resemblance to any persons living or deceased is purely by accident.
No portion of this book reflects any real person or events.

Cover and illustration art by David Cantero
Color assistant, Naiara Fernandez
Managing Art Director, Blake Stephens

Dedicated to Ginger The Dog

June 16, 1999 – May 17, 2013

WE WOULD LIKE TO ACKNOWLEDGE

Our editor: Kathryn Bates

and

Our proofreader: Joey Measel

Table of Contents

Chapter One
Longfellow Makes a Promise

Longfellow lived with Henry, a little old man in a little old house outside of town. Longfellow loved Henry very much, and Henry loved Longfellow just as much in return.

Every morning while they played in the yard, Longfellow would ask, "How much do you love me, Henry?"

At first, Henry would hold his hands just a little way apart and say, "I love you this much, Longfellow."

"Aww, come on, Henry, is that all?" Longfellow would grumble, knowing that Henry was just kidding.

Then Henry would stretch his arms as wide as they would go and say, "I love you this much, Longfellow, and so much more."

This always made Longfellow laugh and laugh. He loved to hear Henry say that.

The best part of the day came just before bedtime. That's when Longfellow would jump into Henry's lap and say, "Could you read me a story, *please*?!"

Henry would reach for the book they had been reading the night before and begin thumbing through the pages. "Now where did we leave off?" To help him find the spot, Longfellow would sniff the pages as Henry turned them. When they came to the page where Henry's scent was the strongest, Longfellow would exclaim, "Right here! Here's where we left off, Henry!"

Henry would nod in agreement and say, "Ah, yes, now I remember," and begin reading from the page Longfellow showed him.

Longfellow would snuggle into Henry's arm and let his imagination soar. If he didn't understand some of the words, Henry would show him the pictures and explain what was going on. Sometimes, just for fun, Henry would put Longfellow into the stories! It was Longfellow, not Toto, who trotted beside Dorothy on the road to Oz. And Longfellow, not Jiminy Cricket, was Pinocchio's best friend.

Longfellow was a good dog and always obeyed Henry. Well except for one lazy summer afternoon. Longfellow had found a cool spot in the meadow and decided to take a nap. From far away, he heard Henry calling him – *Longfellow, come! Come Longfellow!* Longfellow knew he should get up and go to Henry. He even mumbled to himself, "Get moving, legs. Time to run home." But the grass was so soft, and the dirt smelled so sweet; he just let himself drift down, down, down into his dreams.

When he awoke, it was already nighttime. The moon and the stars overhead were casting silvery shadows across the field. "What happened?" Longfellow stammered, jumping to his feet and shaking the sleep from his head.

"Why didn't I run home when Henry called?" he asked himself. "What if Henry has already locked the door and gone to bed? It would be all my fault!" But as Longfellow ran to the house, panting and out of breath, there was Henry on the porch waiting for him.

As soon as Henry saw Longfellow, he pulled himself up from his rocker and hobbled toward him as fast as his limp would allow. "Longfellow, where have you been?" he asked, his voice quivering even more than usual.

Too ashamed to answer, Longfellow lowered his tail and braced himself for a scolding, even though Henry had never ever scolded him before.

Imagine Longfellow's surprise when Henry bent over, scooped him up in his arms, and hugged him to his chest. *"You're okay; you're okay. My prayers have been answered,"* he whispered in Longfellow's ear. "I've been so worried about you! Didn't you hear me calling?" Longfellow couldn't lie to his friend. "Yes, Henry, I heard you, but I was so sleepy, I couldn't walk another step."

"I was afraid you had wandered off into the deep and hidden woods," said Henry. Longfellow perked up his ears. "What deep and hidden woods, Henry? Where are they?" he asked. "Oh, hereabouts," Henry answered nervously, as if he didn't want to talk about them.

"Are there good things or bad things in the deep and hidden woods?" Longfellow asked, growing more and more excited. "I don't rightly know," said Henry as he put Longfellow back on the ground. "Let's explore them together!" Longfellow pleaded. "I'll protect you from the bad things, Henry! I promise!" But Henry didn't answer.

Longfellow was so happy Henry wasn't angry with him. But when he took a closer look at Henry, his little heart sank. "What's wrong, Henry? You're shaking all over."

"Oh, it's nothing Longfellow, just a little chill."

But Longfellow knew better. Henry was shaking because he was old, and because he had been so worried about him disappearing like that.

That very day Longfellow decided to make a solemn wiener dog promise that he would always come when he was called. A solemn wiener dog promise is *not* made lightly. It is, in fact, the most sacred promise any wiener dog can make. Behind it stands all of the faithfulness of all of the wiener dogs that have ever been loved by humans. That makes it nearly impossible to break.

Longfellow stacked his favorite books in a tall pile and placed his front right paw on top of them and said, *I, Longfellow, just a little wiener dog, solemnly promise always to come when Henry calls.*

This was a good promise and Henry seemed pleased, but Longfellow felt it needed something even more to make his solemn promise extra special. He thought of all the wonderful stories Henry had read to him, but nothing came to mind. Finally, after a long pause, Longfellow opened his mouth a second time and out came these words: *I promise now and forever, world without end.*

The hackles on Longfellow's back rose as he said these words. He didn't exactly know what they meant or where they had come from, but they sounded good and brave and noble, and he was very glad he spoke them out loud.

In the weeks that followed, Longfellow roamed the nearby countryside looking for the deep and hidden woods, but he always stayed near enough to home to hear Henry's voice.

No matter how hard he looked though, he was never able to find this mysterious place, and finally he forgot all about it. It would be many years later before he would remember them again.

Chapter Two
Henry Goes Away

Miss O'weeza Tuffy was the county nurse who visited sick people in their homes when they were unable to come to the clinic in town. Every Sunday she would drive out from town to check on Henry and bring groceries from the food bank. When she got there, she would stick what looked like a rubber pull toy in her ears and listen to Henry's heart.

"Now, Henry, your old ticker is not what it used to be," she would say, shaking her head from side to side. "You shouldn't be living out here all alone in this drafty old house without electricity or a telephone."

This always made Longfellow grit his teeth. Henry wasn't alone. He had a brave wiener dog to look after him and keep the bad things away.

Every time Miss Tuffy said this, Henry would cock his head and say, "Now, O'weeza, this has been my home for nearly seventy years. Wild horses couldn't drag me away."

"That's right, you tell her, Henry," Longfellow would say under his breath. He planned to live here with Henry forever and ever. So what if the cold wind sometimes blew through the rafters? He'd just snuggle up closer to Henry, and they'd keep each other nice and warm.

One of Longfellow's earliest memories was of Piggy, the bank that stood on the shelf by the window. Whenever Henry had a few extra coins in his pockets, he'd pull them out and drop them into Piggy.

Longfellow awoke late one night and saw Henry cuddling Piggy in his arms.

"Is Piggy okay?" Longfellow didn't realize that piggy banks can't get sick.

Henry smiled sadly and said, "This money is for you when I go away."

"Where are you going?" Longfellow asked excitedly. He couldn't understand what Henry was saying. He couldn't imagine that Henry would ever go *anywhere* without him.

Two days later, Longfellow was playing with Henry in the yard. Henry threw a stick for him to fetch and off Longfellow ran as happy as could be. He proudly trotted back to Henry with the stick in his mouth, but then something very unusual happened.

Henry bent over and cried out in pain. His knees were shaking too. Something was wrong with Henry. But in a couple of minutes, Henry was able to move again. With his cane to steady him, he walked toward the house.

Longfellow followed Henry into the house. Henry walked to the kitchen and poured three bowls of kibble. He put them on the floor beside Longfellow's water bowl. Longfellow's eyes grew as big as saucers. He had never seen so much food at one time in his whole life.

"Now don't eat it all at once," Henry told him. "This has to last you until Sunday when Miss Tuffy comes. Remember, there's fresh water down at the creek."

Then Henry shuffled slowly toward the bedroom. When he got there, he turned to look at Longfellow. "Always be a good dog," he said, and then he softly closed the door behind him.

Well, what was Longfellow to think? Henry had never closed the door on him before.

That was *his* bedroom, too. He had always slept in there with Henry, right on the bed next to him. Then the answer dawned on him. "Oh of course, how could I be so stupid? Henry is playing a game with me." Longfellow placed his ear against the door and listened for the slightest sound, but there were no sounds to be heard.

"You can come out now, Henry," Longfellow called. "Hide and seek! I found you!"

But Henry didn't come out.

That's when Longfellow began to really worry. "Please come out, Henry!" he begged, scratching at the door with his paws. *"Please come out. I need you."* Then a terrible thought came to Longfellow and filled his heart with dread. There was only one explanation for this. A *bad thing* was in the bedroom with Henry and it wouldn't let him out.

"Come on out, you bad thing!" Longfellow barked, throwing his little body against the door. *"Come on out, I'll fight you! Leave my Henry alone!"* But the bad thing didn't come out. Neither did Henry.

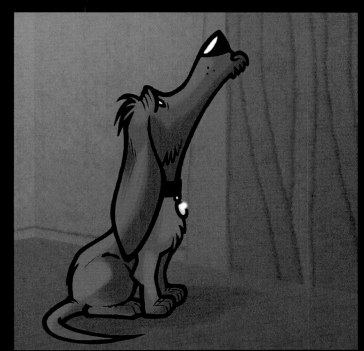

Longfellow stayed by the door all that night and all the next day without even touching his food or water. When Sunday came, he didn't even notice when Miss O'weeza Tuffy drove up in her old jalopy.

As soon as she walked in and saw him curled up against the door like a newborn baby, she cried out, "Oh, my poor dear Longfellow!"

She carried Longfellow to her car and placed him on the front seat. "I'll be right back," she told him.

Longfellow barely knew what was happening because he was so hungry and thirsty.

Miss O'weeza Tuffy returned a little while later with Longfellow's food, water bowl, and toys. "Longfellow, I don't know how to tell you," she began.

"It's okay, Miss Tuffy," Longfellow said quietly, "I know that Henry is gone."

Chapter Three

Longfellow Runs Away

Longfellow's new life with Miss O'weeza Tuffy was very difficult at first. Of course, he was glad he had a place to live, but she wasn't anything like Henry. For a start, she just smelled different.

Longfellow was used to how Henry smelled. He smelled like the outdoors, like the meadow and the creek. Miss Tuffy smelled like soap.

Henry had been full of love and knew how to show it, but Miss O'weeza Tuffy's feelings were locked up inside her.

Miss O'weeza Tuffy kept her house spotlessly clean and expected Longfellow to do the same. He had to wipe his paws on the doormat after he had been digging around in the yard. Henry never made him do that. Miss Tuffy insisted that he not tear up his toys even *after* they lost their squeak! And he was only allowed to lie next to the sofa, never *on* it.

Henry had once read Longfellow the story of Cinderella, and now he was beginning to think Miss O'weeza Tuffy was his wicked stepmother. He had to grit his teeth several times a day to keep from barking at her.

Once, he made the mistake of jumping up on Miss Tuffy when she came in from work. He was just so happy to see her after being left alone all day long, but she said in an angry voice, *"Don't you dare get my uniform dirty, Longfellow!"*

After that, Longfellow was sure she cared more about her uniform than she did about him.

It was the sleeping arrangements that upset Longfellow most of all. He had always slept curled up next to Henry, but Miss O'weeza Tuffy would have none of that. She wouldn't even let him sleep at the foot of the mattress. He had to sleep on the floor!

One afternoon before Miss O'weeza Tuffy got home from work, Longfellow went to the kitchen for some water and spotted something that made his hair stand on end. There, all alone on a shelf, lay Piggy. She was on her side, and there were some coins scattered near her. "Oh, Piggy, you've been robbed!" Longfellow exclaimed, unable to believe his eyes.

This was the piggy that Henry told him would be his someday. And that's when the terrible truth hit Longfellow. Miss O'weeza Tuffy brought him into her home only to get at the money.

Why, she was probably out, that very minute, buying fancy new uniforms for herself…with *his* money.

Longfellow snarled. He wouldn't, he *couldn't* stay with Miss Tuffy a minute longer. There was only one thing to do – he had to run away.

"Be brave," he told Piggy as he gathered the few bits of kibble that were left in his bowl to take with him. "I'll be back for you as soon as I can."

Longfellow tried to hold back his tears as he set out for the train station. He knew that brave and noble wiener dogs never cry. He'd show Miss O'weeza Tuffy. She'd be sorry she hadn't treated him better. He decided he would be a hobo. From now on, he would ride the rails and have grand adventures at every stop.

Longfellow arrived at the station just as the train was pulling in. He ate the last bits of kibble for strength and then looked for a carriage with an open door. He spotted one near the end of the train. He ran as fast as his little legs could carry him. When he got very close, he leapt as high as he had ever leapt in his life. Alas, he landed on the platform with a very hard thud.

"Ouch!" he exclaimed, hurt and confused by the fall. Longfellow realized his wiener legs were just too short to jump on board the train. No amount of trying changed his luck. Longfellow grumbled, as the whistle blew and the train pulled out of the station. "Why wasn't I born a greyhound?"

As darkness began to fall, he heard a rustling in the undergrowth right behind him. A shadowy figure was coming through the bushes and heading straight for him!

"A bear!" Longfellow screamed. *"I'll be eaten alive!"* He was just about to run for his life when he caught a whiff of soap and realized who it was.

"Uh oh, now I'm really in for it," Longfellow thought to himself. He almost wished it *had* been a bear. At least a bear would have ended his miserable life right then and there. Miss O'weeza Tuffy marched right up to Longfellow and towered above him in her white nurse's uniform. "Why did you run away?" she asked. "I've been looking everywhere for you."

"You don't care about me!" he blurted out. "You took me in so you could have all my money, the money Henry saved for me!"

"Is that what you think?" Miss Tuffy asked, falling to her knees and soiling her fine cotton stockings in doing so. "Longfellow, your Henry was the kindest man I have ever known, but he wasn't a rich man. There was barely enough money in Piggy to buy a week's worth of food."

When Longfellow heard that, he hung his head in shame. He was sorry that he had been so unkind to Miss O'weeza Tuffy. She stroked Longfellow's back for the longest time, then gently asked, "I think there is something else you've been holding inside. Isn't it time you let it come out?"

And that's when all the sadness, all the pain, and all the loneliness Longfellow had been feeling since Henry went away came rushing out in a flood of tears. "Oh, Miss Tuffy, I miss him so much!" Longfellow cried. "I want to be with Henry more than anything, but he's not here anymore!"

Miss Tuffy hugged Longfellow's trembling body against her; his muddy feet were getting her uniform all dirty. "I know; I know," she whispered, wiping a tear from his eyes. "I miss him, too, Longfellow."

"I love him so much," Longfellow went on. "Why did he leave me?"

"He didn't want to leave you," Miss Tuffy assured him. "He would have done anything to stay with you, Longfellow, but he couldn't."

"It's all my fault!" Longfellow cried. "I couldn't keep the bad things away!"

"It's *not* your fault," Miss Tuffy said. "Everyone dies one day; it's just the way things are."

Then tears began to fall from Miss O'weeza Tuffy's eyes too. And in that precious moment Longfellow realized something about Miss Tuffy that changed everything. She needed him as much as he needed her.

On the way home, Longfellow's tail began to wag again – not because he wasn't sad anymore, but because he knew he wasn't alone.

Chapter Four
A Big Surprise for Miss Tuffy

As the weeks and months passed, Longfellow settled in at Miss O'weeza Tuffy's house. Even with all the rules and regulations, it was a very nice place to live.

When she was at work, he would curl up in the bathroom near the tub. That's where the soap was that smelled just like her. But these new feelings for Miss Tuffy confused Longfellow. Henry filled his heart completely, and he didn't know if there would be room in there for anyone else.

Late one night, Longfellow awoke to find Miss Tuffy sitting alone in an armchair with only one little candle burning. She was very still. She hardly moved at all. She was almost like a statue. In her hands was a faded old photograph.

After a little while she began to gently rock back and forth and hum a sad song. She stayed there the rest of the night just looking at the photo in her hand and rocking back and forth. As the sun crept through the curtains, Miss Tuffy put the photograph away and got ready for work. Longfellow understood that Miss O'weeza Tuffy missed someone as much as he missed Henry. That's when he decided to do something special for her.

After Miss Tuffy left for work that day, Longfellow gathered up all his toys and set out for town. He decided to sell his toys at the farmers' market and, with the money he'd make, he would treat Miss Tuffy to a surprise celebration. It would do them both good, he thought.

When the owner of the farmers' market saw Longfellow trotting up dragging a bag full of his ragged old toys, he stopped him in his tracks and said, "Sorry, little fellow, we only sell quality merchandise here, and those aren't…" But before he could finish his sentence, every dog at the market was racing toward him. "Mmm…what *is* that delightful smell?" a fluffy Pekingese asked. "I don't think I've ever smelled anything quite like these toys!" A cute little Chihuahua jumped up and down and begged, "Oh, please can I have one?" "How much for the blue one with the stuffing hanging out?" a cranky old bulldog barked.

Longfellow realized these were city dogs who had never smelled good old country toys before. They must have been the most delightful things these dogs had ever smelled. But there was another scent on these toys, one even more irresistible than the scent of the meadow and the creek. It was the scent of Henry's love.

When the sale was over, Longfellow had more than enough money for Miss Tuffy's big surprise.

That evening, when Miss Tuffy got home, Longfellow followed her into the kitchen. He cleared his throat, made a little bow, and asked, "Miss O'weeza Tuffy, would you do me the honor of going out to supper with me this evening?" At first Miss Tuffy hesitated, but when she saw how much it meant to Longfellow, she said, "Why, of course, Longfellow. I'd be honored to go out to supper with you." This made Longfellow so happy that he threw back his head and howled.

Longfellow took Miss O'weeza Tuffy to a little café near the train station. They ate and laughed and laughed and ate until they could eat and laugh no more. When they got home, Miss Tuffy said, "Thank you for such a wonderful supper, Longfellow. I had forgotten how much fun life could be."

Then Miss Tuffy said, "But Longfellow, there is something I must ask you. Where did you get all that money?"

"I sold all my toys at the farmers' market," Longfellow said. "Oh no!" Miss Tuffy exclaimed. "You shouldn't have. They were the only things you had to remember your Henry by. Why did you do it?"

Longfellow said, "You were so sad last night when you were sitting in the armchair all alone and looking at that old photograph. I knew then that you must have loved someone as much as I loved Henry."

"It's true, dear Longfellow, I miss my daughter as much as you miss your Henry. She died many years ago, when she was only a little girl."

"Well, I know what makes the sadness go away, Miss Tuffy!" Longfellow stood on his hind legs and stretched out his front paws as wide apart as they would go, and said, "I love you, Miss O'weeza Tuffy, *this* much and so much more."

Miss Tuffy leaned down and scooped Longfellow up into her arms. Her face beamed with joy. She set Longfellow on her lap and spread her arms as wide as they would go and said, "I love you *this* much, Longfellow, and so much more."

"Now I have something special for you," Miss Tuffy said. "Something from your Henry." Longfellow couldn't believe his ears. "Something from Henry? Really?"

Miss Tuffy left the room and returned with a small wooden box. "Your Henry wanted you to have this when you were grown-up enough to take care of it. I think that time is now." She held the box close to Longfellow's face and opened it slowly.

Longfellow caught his breath. There, just a few inches from his nose, was the medal Henry got when he was a soldier. It used to hang above the fireplace next to a picture of Henry in his uniform when he was a young man. How Longfellow loved that medal! Whenever Henry lit a fire, the medal would catch the light and glow high above him in the shadows.

"How did you get that medal, Henry?" Longfellow once asked. "I got it because of my limp." "I want one, too!" Longfellow pleaded. "No you don't," Henry replied. But he did! And for days after that, Longfellow limped about the house and yard, hoping to get his very own medal. Henry finally had to put a stop to that by telling him, "It's not the limp that gets you the medal. It's how you get the limp."

Now here was Henry's medal, and Miss O'weeza Tuffy was presenting it to him. "Oh, thank you so much, Miss Tuffy!" Longfellow exclaimed, unable to contain his joy. "This is better than a thousand squeaky toys!"

The very next day, Longfellow raced out to the backyard and dug a hole underneath the old oak tree. When he was satisfied that it was deep enough, he dropped in the medal. "I'll never lose it now," he told himself. "It'll always be right here where I've buried it." After covering the hole, Longfellow felt he needed to tell Henry something really important. It took all the courage he could muster. He stood atop the dirt mound and said, "I love Miss O'weeza Tuffy now, Henry. Please don't be mad at me."

Suddenly everything grew still, and then a breeze began to rustle through the oak tree. Longfellow knew it was Henry. Longfellow could hear Henry's familiar voice in the gentle sway of the leaves and branches. "I am so proud of my brave and noble wiener dog," the voice said.

Chapter Five

The Deep and Hidden Woods

The years passed, and Longfellow grew to be a very old dog. His bark wasn't as loud as it used to be and patches of grey appeared on his coat.

"What a distinguished looking gentleman you are," Miss O'weeza Tuffy would tell him, scratching the grey on his chin. "Thank you, Miss Tuffy," he'd reply. "Perhaps we could have minced beef for dinner."

Late one night, Longfellow awoke from a dream. In the dream, he had been digging furiously for something that was buried not in the ground, but deep inside *him*. He had to find it before time ran out, but he couldn't remember what it was.

"The deep and hidden woods," Longfellow mumbled to himself as he was waking. Then he remembered Henry telling him about those woods when he was still a puppy. Suddenly the woods were calling him – pulling him like a magnet, demanding that he come.

Longfellow felt the ancient and mysterious call of the woods in his very bones. He *had* to find them before sunrise, no matter what the cost. It didn't matter that he and Miss O'weeza Tuffy had planned a lovely outing for the morning. The woods were calling and he had to go.

He was careful not to wake Miss Tuffy as he whispered, "Always be happy, Miss O'weeza Tuffy. I must go. The deep and hidden woods are calling me home."

It took all of Longfellow's strength to reach the old homestead before daybreak. Everything looked pretty much the same as it had when he and Henry lived there, except that now tall weeds had overrun the yard. The pull of the woods was very strong here and Longfellow knew he was near his destination.

He started to walk toward the meadow, but then he lost his way. He turned to the east and then to the west. "Where *are* you?" Longfellow called out to the stars.

Something inside him told him to go back to the old house. As he climbed the rickety steps he heard the woods calling from *inside*.

Longfellow pushed open the door with his nose. There, just a few feet away, was the old rocker he and Henry used to sit in when they read books together. Longfellow could almost hear Henry turning the pages. *Now where'd we leave off? Ah, yes, now I remember.*

Longfellow wanted to search every nook and cranny of the house so that he could recall all his precious memories, but his weary old body couldn't take him even one step farther.

"I need to rest," he told himself. "Just for a minute or two." He curled up near the bedroom door where he had last seen Henry and let his eyelids close.

He soon found himself drifting down, down, down – until there was no place left to go. His very last thought was of Henry. Then gently, he was at peace.

And that's when it happened – something wonderful!

If you had been there, you wouldn't have seen it happen, not with your eyes. But maybe, just maybe, you might have seen it with your heart. The bedroom door began to open. Just a crack at first – it could have been the wind. Then it opened a little wider and then a little bit more.

Finally, the door swung open and there stood Henry! He was shining like his medal used to glow in the firelight! And Henry knew just the right words to say, *"Longfellow, come! Come Longfellow!"*

Longfellow remembered the solemn wiener dog promise he made so many years before. He promised to always come when Henry called. And he wasn't about to let a little thing like death stand in his way.

With a yelp of joy, he jumped right out of his body – and into Henry's arms!

Longfellow didn't know what lay ahead in the deep and hidden woods, but the dirt on the path smelled real good, and *Henry* was walking beside him – and that made everything just perfect.

The End

Richard Wagner, M.Div., Ph.D.

Richard is a psychotherapist and has been in private practice since 1981. He lives in Seattle, WA.

David Cantero
Illustrator and cartoonist

Bachelor of Fine Arts, specializing in comics and illustration at the Royal Academy of Fine Arts in Liège, Belgium in 1996.

His varied career, ranging from cartoon to advertising illustration, through editing comic books and children books.

He lives in Barcelona, SPAIN.

53593124R00043

Made in the USA
San Bernardino, CA
21 September 2017